SOME SUN
FLOWERS

A VERY CONTENT
FISH

HAPPY
LADYBUG

To Anna and Marek, my Mom and Dad

Brimming with creative inspiration, how-to projects, and useful information to enrich your everyday life, Quarto Knows is a favorite destination for those pursuing their interests and passions. Visit our site and dig deeper with our books into your area of interest: Quarto Creates, Quarto Cooks, Quarto Homes, Quarto Lives, Quarto Drives, Quarto Explores, Quarto Gifts, or Quarto Kids.

Text and illustrations © 2019 Brayden Kowalczuk
First published in the US in 2021 by First Editions under Frances Lincoln Children's Books,
an imprint of The Quarto Group. 100 Cummings Center, Suite 265D, Beverly, MA 01915, USA.
T +1 978-282-9590 F +1 078-283-2742 www.QuartoKnows.com

A CIP record for this book is available from the Library of Congress.
ISBN 978-0-7112-6264-5
The illustrations were created digitally
Set in Print
Published and edited by Katie Cotton
Designed by Zoë Tucker
Production by Nicolas Zeifman
Manufactured in China CC012021

Brayden Kowalczuk

THE
MOLE
AND THE
HOLE

My name is Mole.
I live here in my hole.

It's my home,
but it's kind of dark
and lonely.

Every day,
I dig, dig,
dig, and
try and leave
this lonely
place.

But when I get to the
top, there's **always**
something blocking
my way.

I don't know what their **problem** is.
When I could go out, all I did was
mind my own business.

I'd **grab** some friends to play,

get in a spot of sunbathing,

. . . DIG!

As I said, I was no trouble
to anyone.

I've tried so many things
to get outside.

Dressing up as a rock...

Telling a funny joke...

...and even pretending there's an earthquake.

"NO MOLES ABOVE GROUND!"

shout the rocks.

Hang on a minute.
What's that light?

"Oh, hey guys."

Phew.

I'm so glad I got away from those rocks.
Wow, this is a great new place to live.
It's got bugs to eat,
places to do my thing,
and this soil's great for digging.

Plus, I can go aboveground
whenever I want.